Becket
wants to be a
priest

Becket R.
Look for the Spirit!

Praying for you
and your domestic
church! Matt K

For our children on earth and in heaven: Mary Clare, Athan,
Becket, Anna Tess, Kieran, Adrian, and Declan.

May God use each of your lives to direct others to the kingdom of heaven.

—Mom and Dad, Authors

For Isabel, Lucia, Cecilia, and Michael Paul.

May you float like feathers on the breath of God.

—Daddy, Illustrator

Cover and interior illustrations by Paul Latino

Text copyright © 2020 by Matt and Stephanie Regitz
Art copyright © 2020 by Paul Latino

Library of Congress Cataloging-in-Publication Data
Names: Regitz, Matt, author. | Regitz, Stephanie, author. | Latino, Paul, illustrator.
Title: Becket wants to be a priest / Matt and Stephanie Regitz; illustrated by Paul Latino.
Description: New York : Paulist Press, 2020. | Summary: "Becket Wants to Be a Priest is a charming children's book about Becket, a regular little boy who goes to school, plays superhero...and wants to be a priest when he grows up"—Provided by publisher.
Identifiers: LCCN 2019056789 (print) | LCCN 2019056790 (ebook) | ISBN 9780809167845 (paperback) | ISBN 9781587687969 (ebook)
Subjects: LCSH: Vocation (in religious orders, congregations, etc.)—Juvenile literature. | Priests—Juvenile literature. | Catholic Church—Clergy—Juvenile literature. | Catholic children—Religious life—Juvenile literature. | Catholic Church—Clergy. sears
Classification: LCC BX2380 .R435 2020 (print) | LCC BX2380 (ebook) | DDC 262/.142—dc23
LC record available at https://lccn.loc.gov/2019056789
LC ebook record available at https://lccn.loc.gov/2019056790

ISBN 978-0-8091-6784-5 (paperback)
ISBN 978-1-58768-796-9 (e-book)

Published by Paulist Press
997 Macarthur Boulevard
Mahwah, New Jersey 07430
www.paulistpress.com

Printed and bound in the
United States of America
By Versa Press, Peoria, Illinois
August 2020

Becket
wants to be a
priest

Matt and Stephanie Regitz

ILLUSTRATED BY Paul Latino

Paulist Press
New York / Mahwah, NJ

My name is Becket. I like playing with my blocks, dressing up like a superhero, and going on adventures outside.

I love my family more than anyone! There's mom and dad, my big brother Athan, my little sister Anna Tess, and my baby brother Kieran. We are all named after saints. Kieran is really cute, but he's always knocking over my blocks!

My family is in church a lot, even when we're not going to Mass. My dad works there, teaching the big kids about God after school. Sometimes Athan, Anna Tess, and I come too, and we get to play games, pray, and listen to my dad's stories about Jesus.

This year, I go to the same school as Athan: Saint Anne's. It's named after Mary's mother. I love my new classroom, and my favorite spot is the prayer corner. When I'm done with my work, I go there with my new friend, Gavin, and we pray together.

I go to Mass two times a week! At school, we go to Mass every Wednesday. I have a Mass buddy, Anthony, who shows me when to stand up and sit down, and what prayers to say.

He's older than me, so I just follow along with him.

I also go to Mass on Sunday with my family. We always sit up front, close to the altar. Sometimes I get tired and fall asleep, but I love singing the songs and watching the priest.

One night at dinner, as my whole family is sitting at the table together, Dad asks us who we want to be when we grow up.

Athan wants to be a soccer player. Anna Tess wants to be a veterinarian. Kieran is still a baby, but we think he'd like to be a zookeeper, because he's always making animal noises! When it's my turn to answer, I tell Dad I want to be a priest.

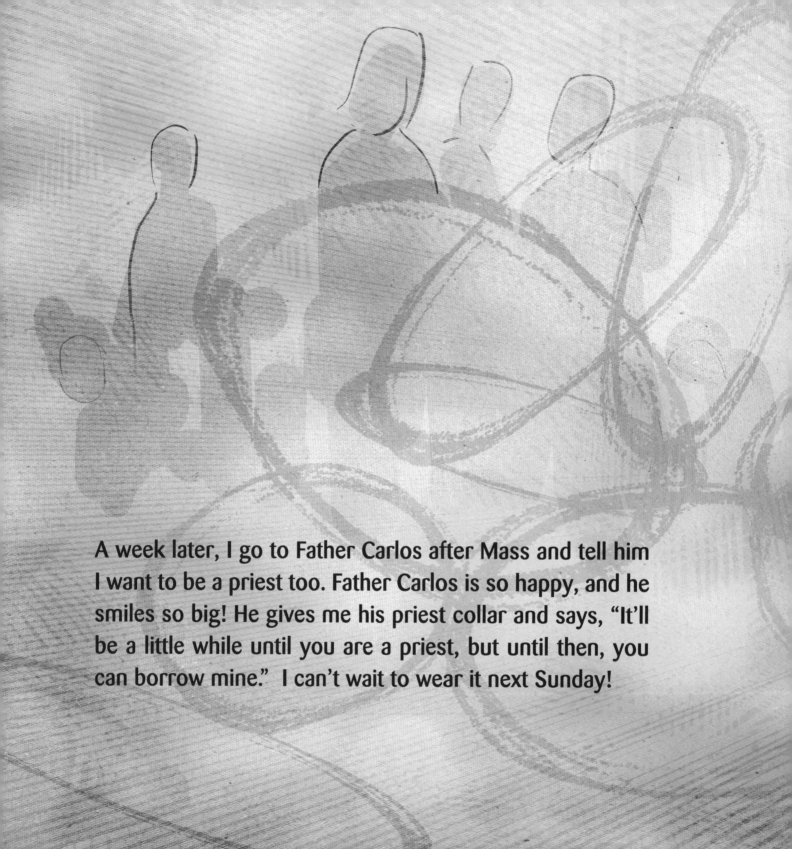

A week later, I go to Father Carlos after Mass and tell him I want to be a priest too. Father Carlos is so happy, and he smiles so big! He gives me his priest collar and says, "It'll be a little while until you are a priest, but until then, you can borrow mine." I can't wait to wear it next Sunday!

For Christmas, I get an even more amazing gift. I run downstairs with Athan and Anna Tess, passing out the presents with our names on it. The biggest one is for me! I open it up, and what is inside…? A Mass kit! It has everything you need to celebrate Mass.

Right away, I put the priest's Mass clothes over my pajamas. Everyone in the house plays a part: Athan does the readings, Anna Tess brings up the gifts, Mom and Dad sit in the pews, and Kieran carries the cross. But all he wants to do is swing it around!

One day in the spring, Mom shows me a fancy envelope addressed to me. What could it be? Father Carlos is inviting us to a big celebration called an ordination. Two guys are going to become priests! Mom helps me write back to Father Carlos, thanking him for inviting us and saying that we'll be there! Dad marks the date on the calendar. I can't wait!

The ordination day is finally here. I wear my nicest clothes and the priest collar that Father Carlos gave me. We go to a huge church called a cathedral. There are so many people here! Dad takes us to sit at the very front so I can see everything. The Mass is long, and there is a special kind of priest there called a bishop, who is in charge of all the other priests.

At the end, when the guys line up to be blessed, *to become priests*, I get so excited! I whisper to my mom, "One day, that'll be ME!"

After the Mass, we all go to a big party with the new priests. There's lots of food and lots of cake for me!

Soon it's time to go home, and time to go to bed. Before we go to sleep, Mom and Dad pray with us. But tonight, Dad asks me to lead. "Thank you, God, for such a good day," I say, "and God, please make me a priest when I grow up."

After Mom and Dad tuck me into bed, I feel something warm near my heart that spreads to the tips of my fingers and puts a smile on my face. I feel God's love for me!

Tomorrow, I'll play Mass again, and maybe build a church with my favorite blocks. I sure hope Kieran won't knock it over again this time!

Becket is guided by the Holy Spirit all through the story. Can you find the feathers the Holy Spirit left behind?